THE CASE OF THE
CAR-BARKAHOLIC DOG

THE CASE OF THE
CAR-BARKAHOLIC DOG

John R. Erickson

Illustrations by Gerald L. Holmes

Maverick Books
Published by Gulf Publishing Company
Houston, Texas

Maverick Books
Published by Gulf Publishing Company
P.O. Box 2608, Houston, Texas 77252-2608

10 9 8 7 6 5 4 3 2

Library of Congress Cataloging-in-Publication Data

Erickson, John R., 1943–
    The case of the car-barkaholic dog / John R. Erickson ;
illustrations by Gerald L. Holmes.
        p.   cm. — (Hank the Cowdog ; 17)
    "Maverick books."
    Issued also on cassette.
    Summary: Hank the Cowdog, Head of Ranch Security, finds himself
stranded in town and drawn into a dangerous situation involving his
sister Maggie and a terrible bully named Rambo.
    ISBN 0-87719-198-0 — ISBN 0-87719-199-9 (pbk.). — ISBN
0-87719-200-6 (cassette)
    1. Dogs—Fiction.   [1. Dogs—Fiction.   2. West (U.S.)—Fiction.
3. Humorous stories.]   I. Holmes, Gerald L., ill.   II. Title.
PS3555.R428C36   1991
[Fic]—dc20   91-13844
                                                            CIP
                                                            AC

Printed in the United States of America

Cover design by Tom Hair

Hank the Cowdog is a registered trademark of John R. Erickson.

CONTENTS

CHAPTER
1

ON THE DILEMMAS
OF A HORN

I t's me again, Hank the Cowdog. It was in the fall of the year, seems to me. Yes, it was.

October. Warm days, cool nights, the chinaberries and elms showing the first colors of fall. And we'd just gotten in two truckloads of steers the week before.

Busy time on the ranch, getting all those steers straightened out and ready to go out on wheat pasture. I'd been up day and night with those steers, and it had just about worn me down.

I mean, overwork comes with the territory when you're Head of Ranch Security. You expect it. Still, a guy needs a rest once in a while, a break from all the cares and responsibilities of running the ranch.

I needed the rest, yes, but the rest of what followed the rest I didn't need at all. Little did I know that I would find myself stranded in town, or that I would be drawn into a dangerous situation involving my sister Maggie and a terrible bully named Rambo.

But that's getting the kettle before the pot. We had received all these fresh cattle and we had a bunch of scrubs in the sick pen. I kind of like that sick-pen work. Some of us are born to take care of the sick and unfirmed, the crippled, and the lame. Not me. I was born to give 'em orders.

What we do, see, is drive the steers into the crowding pen and shut the gate on them. Then we run, oh, seven or eight of them into the alley that leads to the doctoring chute.

You ever see a top-of-the-line, blue-ribbon cowdog handle cattle in an alley? Very impressive. While the cowboys have a steer in the chute, I march up and down the alley, growling at the cattle and letting them know who's running the show.

Usually that's all it takes to make the deal run smooth. 'Course, every now and then we get one that's new to the sick pen and doesn't know how to follow orders, and that's when I earn my pay. I have 37 different ways of biting reluctant steers to make 'em move.

Yes, every once in a while I get kicked on the
nose, but success is never free.

We made a pretty good team, me and the cowboys, and it didn't take us long to run twelve
head through the chute. I might point out,
though, that while we were working, Little
Drover sat over by the water tank. Goofing off.

That little mutt can find more ways to kill time and lollygag around than any dog I ever knew. For a while he watched the action, and now and then he would add his "yip-yip-yip." Then he chewed on an old horn he'd found in the lot, and after he'd chewed on it for a while, he dug a hole and buried it — shoveled the dirt over it with his nose.

Why did he want to bury a horn? Beats me.

Well, when I'd finished my work and while the cowboys were putting up the medicine, I swaggered over to the water tank, where Mister Half-Stepper was licking on a piece of ice.

"Eating Popsicles on the job, huh?"

He grinned and wagged his stub tail. "Yeah. They're pretty good. You want one?"

"No, I don't want one. Maybe I'm old-fashioned, Drover, but somehow the idea of eating Popsicles on the job strikes me wrong. Where I come from, we do the work first and then we goof off."

"I sure agree with that."

"Then why don't you show it with your actions?"

"I do. I always let you do the work first."

"That's exactly what I mean. Is there some reason why you don't jump in and try to make a hand when we're doctoring cattle?"

"Oh yeah. Last time I tried it, I got kicked."

"You got kicked. Son, getting kicked is just part of the job. It happens all the time."

"I know. And it always hurts."

"Of course it hurts, but our ability to tolerate pain is one of the things that makes cowdogs just a little bit special."

He rolled his eyes up at the clouds. "Seems to me that the best way to tolerate pain is not to get kicked."

I moved closer and glared at him. "Are you saying that the best way to tolerate pain is to avoid it? What if I took that attitude? How long do you think this ranch would run without pain?"

"I don't know."

"About five minutes. Pain is our fuel, Drover. It's the force that drives us. It's pain that lets us know that we're alive. To run from pain is to run from life."

"Sounds like a pretty good idea to me."

I could only shake my head. "All right, you leave me with no choice. Just for that, I'll have to write you up. For making dumb remarks about pain, you get three Shame-On-You's on your record."

"Oh gosh. That hurts."

"Exactly. Which just goes to prove my point that you can't escape pain, no matter how hard you try. Now, why did you bury that horn?"

"Which horn?"

"The horn you just buried."

"Oh, that horn. Well, I don't know. I guess I wanted to save it. You never know when you might need a horn."

"So far so good, Drover, but that brings us to the most important question of all. *Now that you've buried it, can you find it?*"

His eyes blanked out. "Well, I think I can."

I sat down and gave him a wise smile. "Prove it. Find the horn."

He went to several spots, pawed around in the dirt, and came up with exactly nothing. He came padding back, sat down, scratched his ear, and said, "I guess I've lost it."

"Exactly!" I leaped to my feet and began pacing around him. This was a triumphal moment, don't you see. "Now let me tie all this together into one Lesson For The Day, Drover. You ran from pain but found it. You found a horn but lost it. That which you tried to save you have no more, but that which you tried to lose you have. Do you see what this means?"

"Not really."

Suddenly it occurred to me that I didn't know what it meant either, except that it meant something very important. But even more important

6

was that I overheard Slim and Loper talking. They had just stepped out of the medicine shed.

"We're out of Pen-Strip and Furison," said Loper, "and we'll need both in the morning. While you're at the feed store, pick up four hundred pounds of horse feed. And stop at the Waterhole and get me a pouch of Taylor's Pride chew."

Slim was writing all this down in the palm of his hand. "Okay, is that all?"

"Stay out of the pool hall and get back out here as soon as you can. We've got two weeks' work to finish up before dark."

Slim nodded. "Seems kind of a waste, making a trip into town and not stopping at the pool hall."

"You can handle it."

"Well, I don't know." Slim looked up at the sky and rubbed the whiskers on his cheek. "There's something about that pool hall, Loper. I mean, a lot of times that old pickup just heads there on its own and I can't hold it in the road."

"Hold it in the road and get back out here."

"Loper, has anyone ever told you that you ain't any fun?"

"All the time. It comes from working poor help."

Slim smiled and they drifted towards the

flatbed pickup. "Shoot! You've got the finest cowboy crew in the whole world."

I didn't hear the rest of the conversation, which was okay because it was starting to get a little windy. The conversation, that is.

Also, I had gleaned enough information by that time to conclude A) that Slim was going into town; B) that I hadn't been to town in quite a spell; C) that I needed a change in scenery; and D) that Slim probably wanted me and Drover to go along and ride shotgun.

I turned to my assistant. "Drover, a pickup is fixing to go into town, and we're fixing to sneak our little selves into the back end and hitch a ride. Let's go."

Drover had stopped and put his nose to the ground. Then his head came up.

"I found the horn, Hank, it's right here where I left it. Does that change your Lesson For The Day?"

I gave him a withering glare. "I deal in concepts, son. What actually happens just confuses the issue. Come on, we've got a ride to catch."

CHAPTER
2

SYRUPTISHUS
LOADERATION

I n the Security Business, we have special techniques for special jobs. Your ordinary dogs know nothing of these special techniques because it takes a special kind of dog to apply special techniques. Ordinary dogs use ordinary techniques.

And to no one's surprise, they usually fail.

We have special techniques for catching mice in the cake house. We have special techniques for dealing with chickens. We have special techniques for humbling cats, and special techniques for dodging the rocks that ranch wives, upon hearing their cats being humbled, tend to throw at dogs.

And we have special techniques for hitching rides into town. The technical term for this procedure is "Syruptishus Loaderation." Quite a term, huh? I get a kick out of using heavyweight terms every now and then. 'Course, I don't expect everyone to remember them, and I won't take the time to . . .

Oh, what the heck? We might as well take a short break and have ourselves a little lesson in words, their origins, and their many shades of meaning.

After all, language is pretty important. Without language, we'd all be at a loss for words.

Okay. "Syrup-tish-us Load-er-a-tion." It means, "A secret and rather technical procedure for climbing aboard a pickup that is heading for town, when the driver of the alleged pickup would be less than thrilled if he knew that he was hauling dogs."

You'll notice that the root of the first word is "syrup." Perhaps you've observed the way that syrup moves. It doesn't run or fall or hop or splash. It *oozes* along its course, which is a sneaky and stealthy way of moving.

Things that ooze, such as snakes and snails, are usually up to no good, and by simple logic it follows that most of your syrups are up to no good. Hence, from the root "syrup," we build a new and exciting word that means "sneaky and stealthy."

The root of the second word is "load." If you've ever loaded roots, you know that they can be very heavy, especially if they're packed in gunny-sacks and if they have to be lifted from ground level up to the bed of a pickup.

Hence, from the second load we find that roots are a major cause of back injury and . . .

I seem to have lost my train of thought. Some-thing about roots. Or trees. Tree roots?

Oh well, you get the picture. "Syruptishus load-eration." You might want to jot that one down.

Okay. Now we'll give our new term a practical application from Real Life. Loper went on about his business, and Slim headed for the pickup, which was parked directly in front of our bed-room under the gas tanks.

I gave Drover a secret sign which meant "Switch to Stealthy Crouch Mode and follow Slim." Because of the highly secret nature of the secret sign, I'm not at liberty to reveal it at this time.

Nothing personal. It's just that there are parts of this job that too sensitive to be revealed to the general public. If our codes were ever broken

. . . well, I'm not at liberty even to suggest what might happen if our codes fell into the wrong hands.

We switched over to Stealthy Crouch Mode, fell into formation behind Slim, and began secretly and stalkingly stealthing him. At the same time, my Data Control began loading the Syruptishus Loaderation program, and I began going through my checklist of procedures and routines.

I know it sounds complicated. It sounds complicated because it IS complicated. And now you understand that being a ranch dog is no ball of wax.

Slim walked up to the pickup and stopped. Taking our cues from the visual readout of his movement, we stopped too. Or, to be more precise, I stopped and Drover ran into me.

"Ooops, 'scuse me."

"Shhh, quiet! Pay attention to your business."

"Sorry."

"Shhhhh!"

"Sorry."

"SHHHHHHHHH!"

"'Scuse me."

"Will you shut your little trap!"

"I'm sorry, Hank."

"SHUT UP!"

"Okay." At last, silence. But then, "I'm sorry."

I could have . . . but wringing his stupid neck at that particular moment would have only created more of a stir, and that was precisely what we didn't need.

"We're in Stealthy Crouch Mode, you little dunce, and I don't want to hear another word out of you."

"Okay."

"That's better."

I turned my attention back to Slim. Hmmm. He appeared to be removing the lid from the pickup's gas tank and placing the nozzle of the gas tank hose into the gas tank. In other words, he appeared to be . . . yes. Filling the pickup with . . . well, gas.

Or, to be more precise, gasoline. There are many types of gas floating around in our atmosphere, but only one type of gasoline: regular and unleaded. That's two, actually.

And gasoline doesn't float. It moves from one tank to another through a hose and a nozzle and so forth.

I hadn't expected this turn of events. It takes your average cowboy several minutes to fill the gas tank of his pickup, and I don't need to tell you how difficult it is for a dog to maintain Stealthy Crouch Mode over a period of several minutes.

It's tough. It wears you out. Your ordinary dogs will break discipline at this point. Your better dogs will maintain S.C.M., whatever the cost.

Slim was tapping his toe and singing a song, as he waited for the tank to fill.

Doe dee doe doe doe,
Dee dee deedle dum
Doe dee doe doe
Diddle diddle diddle dum.

Ho fiddly diddly dum
Hey diddle riddly rum
Diddly riddly fiddly fum
Doe dee dee, dee diddly dum.

Pretty boring song, if you ask me. I could have come up with a better one — blindfolded and with one paw tied behind my back.

Well, Mr. Songbird got so involved in singing his masterpiece that he forgot that he was filling the pickup with gas. And you can guess what happened. The tank filled up and gasoline went flying in all directions.

That woke him up. "DAD-gum gas tank! Now look what you've done. Stupid pickup."

He hung the nozzle back on its special patented

baling wire hook and scowled at his hands. For a moment he stood there muttering to himself. It appeared that he considered wiping them on his jeans but changed his mind.

It was then that his gaze fell upon me.

"Hank, come here, boy. Good dog. Come on, boy."

HUH?

I, uh, tried to blend in with my surroundings, so to speak, in hopes that he might . . .

"Hank, come here!" The softer tone of his first call had disappeared, replaced by a certain sharp quality. "Come here!"

"Drover," I whispered, "you're being called for special duty. Slim needs you."

There was no answer. I turned around and . . . I don't know how that little dope always manages to . . .

"HANK, GET OVER HERE!"

I swallowed and pushed myself up to the Full Erect Position.

"Come on, hurry up!"

I began the slow walk towards the pickup. There are some parts of this job that I have never learned to enjoy.

"Come on, atta boy."

I hate the smell of gasoline, always have.

"Come on, pooch, I've got places to go."

There are times when a dog's loyalty to the ranch is put under a terrible strain.

"There we go. Come here. Good dog."

I sat down at his feet, wagged my tail, and gave him my most wounded look. Perhaps if I . . .

He wiped his hands on my back. That much came as no surprise. But then he SCRUBBED HIS FINGERNAILS ON MY EARS!

That really hurt my pride. That was a low blow. I mean, a guy spends hours and hours cleaning himself up and trying to keep up the kind of neat personal appearance that you'd expect in a Head of Ranch . . .

"Good dog, Hankie."

Two pats on the head and goodbye, Charlie.

In many ways, this is a lousy job, and I made up my mind then and there that if I ever got my paws on Drover . . .

He climbed into the pickup and started the motor. Slim did, not Drover. Drover had jumped into a hole and pulled in behind him, the dunce, the backstabbing little . . .

The pickup pulled away from the gas tanks. I had not a moment to spare, for the moment of truth had arrived.

In a flash, I switched from Wounded Dog Mode over to Syruptishus Loaderation Mode. I began oozing along behind the pickup and slipped into the blind spot — the spot near the hitch ball, which just happened to be outside the view of the side mirrors, ho ho.

That's why we call it the Blind Spot, because the driver can't see back there, don't you see.

As the pickup gathered speed, I initiated the countdown.

Three.

Two.

One.

Blastoff, liftoff, bonzai, charge!

As graceful as a deer, I launched myself from the caliche drive in front of the house and landed on silent paws in the back end of the pickup. Don't know as I had ever done the procedure any better, and Slim never suspected a thing.

And so it was that I smuggled myself onto the pickup bed and hitched a ride into town. Yes, I did smell of gasoline, and yes, my personal appearance had taken a serious blow.

But it could have been worse. Consider the wind, for example. It blows all the time.

RUNNING THE EIGHTEEN-WHEELER MARATHON

I enjoyed the ride into town. Sitting on the spare tire, I closed my eyes and let the wind blow my ears around.

At last, serenity. Peace and quiet. All the heavy responsibility of running the ranch slipped away as if by magic, and I surrendered myself to the touch of the wind.

Did I get cold back there? Yes, somewhat. But that was a small price to pay for the peace and quiet and tranquility and so forth.

I did encounter one test of my willpower on the way to town. We had just left the caliche road and gotten on the main highway, when all

at once a big cattle truck came up out of nowhere, blew his horn, and passed us.

That tested me, sure did. See, I don't like trucks in the first place, and I like 'em even less when they blow their horns at me and play big shot. And this one was hauling cattle and it's real hard for me not to bark at cattle.

The temptation to give that guy a severe barking was almost overpowering, yet I knew in my heart of hearts that if I barked, I would reveal my presence in the back of the pickup. I didn't know what Slim might do if he discovered me back there, and I wasn't real keen on finding out, because among his choices was throwing me out and letting me walk home.

So I ground my teeth together and glared daggers at the truck and let him off without a barking. But I vowed right then and there that if me and that truck ever met again, he would get a double treatment. Or even a triple treatment.

He'd sure regret blowing his horn at Hank the Cowdog, because Hank the Cowdog does not take trash off a truck, not even a trash truck.

Well, after a few minutes of breathing his diesel smoke and choking down my anger, I got control of myself and tried to enjoy the rest of the trip.

Then all at once, the pickup began to slow and the whine of the mudgrips moved into a different key. I looked out and saw that we were stopping at Waterhole 83.

Slim got out, dusted the alfalfa leaves off the front of his shirt, stomped some mud off of his boots, rearranged his hat so that it rode at a rakish angle, flicked the toast crumbs out of his beard, wiped his nose on the sleeve of his shirt, and went swaggering inside.

When a cowboy goes to all that trouble to fix

himself up, you know it's a special occasion. Stopping at the Waterhole was pretty special.

Well, I waited and I waited. You know about me and waiting. I hate it. Some dogs can sit in the back of a pickup for hours and hours, and it doesn't seem to bother them. Me? I get bored. It's hard for an active mind . . .

Wasn't that the same cattle truck that had passed us out on the highway? Red Kenworth, chrome stacks, a hairy little stuffed monkey hanging from the sun visor. By George yes! Same outfit. And now we knew why he'd been in such a big rush and why he'd been blowing everybody off the road.

Coffee time at the Waterhole.

I threw a glance inside and saw Slim sipping on a cup of coffee and talking to another cowboy. He'd be another thirty minutes getting out the door.

I hopped down to the pavement and sort of casually made my way over towards the truck. Before I made any serious moves, see, I wanted to make sure that the driver had gone inside.

I circled the rig and, just as I had suspected, the guy had been foolish enough to leave his entire truck unguarded.

Having established this, I dropped all attempts

to disguise my behavior and rushed forward. I reached the left front tire, sniffed it twice, and blasted the center out of that pretty chrome hub. I mean, it was a bull's eye.

From there, I moved on down to the driver wheels on the left side, knocked them out, and kept going, gathering speed as I went along. I made the turn at the bottom end of the trailer, knocked out four axles' worth of tires at the back, and headed for the tandem driver wheels on the right side.

The procedure couldn't have gone any smoother. I mean, we're talking about world-class speed. I wasn't keeping my time on this deal, but I had a feeling that I'd done the entire left side in something like 00:48.5 seconds.

As I recalled, my uncle Beanie, one of the fastest tire dogs who ever lived, had once run an eighteen-wheeler in 1:58.7, with a first leg of 00:51.3. In other words, I had me a record going here, if I could keep up the pace.

The toughest part of the Eighteen-Wheeler Marathon comes after you do the trailer tires and sprint for the second set of driver wheels. It's a long run, and by that time a guy has begun to wear down. It's a real test of fitness and training and endurance.

Most dogs can't handle it. They'll run out of zip on the straightaway, and a lot of 'em will sit down and rest.

I was tempted to rest. I mean, I'm only flesh and blood, bones and hair and toenails, two eyes, two ears, and did I ever mention that the women-folk really do handsprings when they see my nose?

I'm not one to boast, but some very important authorities on noses have singled out MINE as one of the finest, if not THE finest, noses in the entire Northern Cowdog District of Texas.

Where was I? Something about . . . kind of got distracted there. Huh. Just lost it.

Oh yes, the Eighteen-Wheeler Hurdles Marathon. It's a toughie, and as I was saying, your ordinary dog begins to give out after he rounds the curve at the rear of the trailer and hits that long straightaway. Many are tempted to stop and rest, and in fact, most DO stop and rest.

Me? I was tempted, but I had a feeling that I had me a record-breaker going, if I could just gut it out and keep running. Did I stop and rest? No sir. I ignored the burning lungs, the weakened legs, the terrible dehydration, and all the rest of the physical symptoms of physical exhaustion, and plunged onward to the next set of tires.

Gasping for breath, I reached the driver wheels

on the right side, came to an abrupt stop, lifted my left leg, and . . .

"Get away from my truck, you flea bag!"

EEEEEEEEEEE-YOWW!!

You ever been buzzed with a hot shot?

Truck drivers often carry a device called a hot shot, see. It's a long plastic thing with batteries in the handle and two evil little prongs on the end. They use the hot shot to improve the get-along of cattle when they're going in and out of a cattle truck.

Apply that same wicked device to an innocent dog who is minding his own business and you will see an incredible display of gymnastics, acrobatics, and hieroglyphics.

Okay. This smart aleck truck driver, this brute, this practical joker must have come out of the Waterhole, and perhaps he had just loaded his hot shot with fresh batteries. Yes, I'm sure he had.

And he saw me there, minding my own business, hurting no one, making no noise, and causing this world not one bit of trouble or grief. In fact, I was on the point of shattering the World Record in the Eighteen-Wheeler Hurdles Marathon.

And what did he do? He buzzed me with his hot shot, fresh batteries and all, buzzed me in a moment of weakness and vulnerablity, buzzed me for absolutely no reason except that he thought it would be fun to see a poor dog do three and a half flips in the air and come apart at the seams.

Very funny.

Just for that, I left his dumb old truck. By George, if he couldn't act any better than that, I would just win my World Record on somebody's else's truck. Hey, there were lots of trucks in the world, and most drivers would have . . .

He didn't deserve the honor and glory, and I didn't like his stupid old . . .

I left out of there in a big hurry, zoomed around the back side of the Waterhole, and didn't slow down until I had taken refuge, so to speak, behind the north side.

There, I caught my breath and tried to lick down the hair on my back, which was sticking up like a stiff-bristle brush. That done, I peeked around the northeast corner of the building and did a visual scan of the parking lot, just to be . . .

HUH?

Slim and the pickup were pulling out on the highway. My ranch's pickup was . . . Slim had . . . how could he . . . but of course he hadn't known . . .

He was gone and there was no stopping him.

I was stranded, fellers. I had been abandoned in town.

You probably think that my next move was to go back around to the south side of the Waterhole and physically attack that smart-aleck truck driver.

Good guess. Yes, I thought about it, long and hard. But after thinking about it long and hard, and I mean doing some heavy-duty soul searching of my soul, I came to the realization that the guy should be pitied.

Tearing off one of his legs wouldn't make him a better human bean. It would only lead both of us into a spiral of anger and bitterness.

The measure of a dog lies in his ability to forgive and forget.

I decided to forgive him for being such an idiot, and not to forget that he still had that hot shot and might use it on me again if I showed myself.

So, with that weight off my conscience, I hugged the north wall of the Waterhole and waited until I saw his stupid, stinking, rattletrap of a junk-heap truck pull out on the highway.

Then, and only then, did I step out and give him a withering barage of barking. And like all louts and cowards throughout history, he drove away as fast as he could — utterly shaken by my display of moral superiority.

Hey, if you're on the side of Right, you're on the side of Might and you don't need to Bite.

But a little barking never hurts a thing.

CHAPTER
4

CHICKEN BONES BRING
NEW MEANING TO LIFE

So there I was, stranded in town. That might have bothered me if it hadn't been for the fact that I had dozens of friends with whom I could . . .

Several friends. A few. Did I have any friends in Twitchell?

Okay, maybe I didn't, but I did have kinfolks — my very favorite sister, Maggie. And if you've got kinfolks, who needs friends?

It had been quite a while since I'd paid a visit to Maggie and her four lovely children, and to be honest about it, I felt a little guilty about that. I mean, a guy can get so wrapped up in his work that he neglects his kinfolks, and I happened to

29

know that Mag had always, well, kind of idolized me.

I owed her a visit, so I just said, "What the heck, I'll take the time to check in on Maggie and the kids." I left the Waterhole, hit Main Street, and followed it into town.

It was almost dark by the time I reached her neighborhood, and I figgered I had better find her place while there was still enough light to find it.

I'd only been there once before, you see, and although the chances of me getting into the wrong yard were very remote, in the Security Business we never rule out any possibility, no matter how remote.

Okay. I pointed myself towards the north and made my way to the end of the street. There, I hung a right turn, trotted some twenty yards to the east, made another right, and found myself in the alley.

Ah! Immediately I felt more comfortable. I've always been more of an alley-guy than a front-street-guy (maybe I've already said that but it never hurts to emphasize important points), and I've always felt more at home amongst garbage barrels and gas meters than amongst shrubs and pretty lawns.

Yes, all at once I felt at ease, trotting along in the ruts of the garbage truck, and ... hmmmm.

I stopped and lifted my nose and sampled the air. A fresh and exciting aroma was riding the evening breeze, and unless I was badly mistakened, it had something to do with fried chicken.

Fried chicken bones just happened to be one of my all-time favorite foods.

I locked in on the scent and followed it ten paces to the northeast and found myself standing in front of a silver garbage barrel. I glanced up and down the alley and, seeing no one, hopped up on my back legs, hooked my front paws over the lip of the barrel, and pulled it over on its side.

My, my! Delicious aromas came pouring out of the barrel, as well as a few sundry items such as old newspapers, milk cartons, letters, bills, cans, bottles, and so forth.

I began a Sniffing and Digging Procedure, checking out each item for goodies. Those items that failed to test out positive for goodies, I shoveled outside the barrel. Through hard work and careful examination, I was able to narrow down the material to a single bundle of something wrapped in a newspaper, which had rested near the bottom of the barrel before it had, uh, fallen over, so to speak.

G.L. Holmes

Yes, this was it! With paws and teeth, I slashed at the outer wrapping of paper, and at last . . . mercy! Fried chicken bones, oh how I love them!

The leg bones crunch so nicely. The end-portion of the wings and the rib section can often be counted upon to have some crust left on them. And you can almost always find two juicy strips of meat that have been left on either side of the backbone.

Have we ever done the Chicken Bone song? Maybe not, but we certainly should. Here goes:

The Chicken Bone Blues

Late in the evening, the sun's gone down
A country dog finds himself in town,
Singing a song called the Chicken Bone Blues.

Walk down the alley, go through the trash,
Looking for a treasure, and I don't mean cash.
Singing a song called the Chicken Bone Blues.

Sometimes this old world treats you badly.
It's filled with sorrow, pain, and strife.
But then you find a whole new meaning in the
    alley of life.
You pick through the garbage and you don't
    have to beg,
Just dig 'till you find a chicken leg.

I had me a woman, heart was of stone,
I'm giving my love to a chicken bone.
Singing a song called the Chicken Bone Blues.

The women'll say they don't need you,
A garbage can will always feed you.
Singing a song called the Chicken Bone Blues.

I'm not looking for someone's pity
But I think I'll put my heart up on the shelf.
There's not much to be gained feeling sorry
   for myself.
When it comes to bones, I am Aristotle.
When it's time to eat, I can hit the throttle.

The sun's gone down, the alley's dark.
I'm just as happy as a finger-licking lark.
Singing a song called the Chicken Bone Blues.

For every woman, there's a man.
For every dog, there's a garbage can.
Singing a song called the Chicken Bone Blues,
Oh yeah,
Singing a song called the Chicken Bone Blues.

Needless to say, I dived in and had myself an old-fashioned garbage-barrel feast.

There is an ancient rumor, based on incorrect information, that dogs cannot or should not eat chicken bones, because . . . something foolish, such as that dogs will choke on . . .

COUGH! WHEEZE! ARG!

Hmmm. It appeared that something had caught in my throat. Probably a shred of newspaper or perhaps a coffee ground or . . .

COUGH! WHEEZE! ARG!

Must have been a shred of newspaper. You

see, newspaper will lump up and get caught in the. . . .

It wouldn't go down, no matter how hard I tried to swallow it. Nor would it come back up.

One of the dangers of feasting in garbage cans is that a guy runs some risk of ingesting lumps of newspaper which . . .

COUGH! WHEEZE! ARG! ULP!

This was no good. Obviously, I had bitten into some tainted lumps of newspaper and my best course of action lay in finding some water to wash them down. Before I strangled.

Hence, I cancelled the feast, backed out of the garbage barrel, and made my way past all the litter and trash. What a mess! It was shocking to see how little some people cared about the appearance of their alley. Trash was everywhere!

You know me, I'm no fussbudget, but still, if I had an alley behind my house — which I don't because I don't have a house, the cowboys won't build a house for their Head of Ranch Security, that tells you what a cheap-John outfit I work for — and where was I?

Oh yes, trash and litter. If I had a house in town with an alley behind it, I think I'd take a little more pride in the appearance of my alley than some people I could mention.

But never mind all that because I had more

serious problems to attend to than a messy alley. I had a b . . . a lump of newspaper hung up in my throat, windpipe, food tube, esophocles, whatever you call that thing, and I sure needed a drink of water to wash it down.

Hence, I hurried down the alley to find my sister's yard.

In the dark, all back fences begin to look pretty muchly alike.

It had been a while, see. I had only been there once before. It was very dark. I was in a hurry. Who wouldn't have been in a hurry?

What I'm driving at is that I made three passes up and down the stupid alley and couldn't decide which yard belonged to my sister, and all the while that chicken . . . that chicken-flavored news-paper lump was dealing me misery.

But at last, on the fourth pass, my recollection of the place began to return and I had narrowed my choices down to two: Yard A and Yard B.

Which was it? I had to make a choice. Making important choices while coughing and gagging and wheezing is not easy, but I had to do it.

So I made the choice, and perhaps you'd be interested in knowing how I went about it. Okay, you asked. Here goes.

At first glance, a guy would be inclined to

choose A over B, because A comes first in the alphabet, can be divided by 2, and somehow just looks more appealing than a B, I don't know why.

On second glance, a guy would be even more inclined to choose A over B because B sounds a lot like "bee" and bees sting. Nobody has ever been stung by an "A" or by anything that even resembled an A.

But on third glance and on the other hand, if a guy is inclined to be superstitious, he knows that Life plays tricks on all of us. Oftentimes what appears to be obvious is only a fake and a fraud, a mean trick played upon us by whoever it is that plays tricks and enjoys watching us mess up.

Hencely, a shrewd mind will make the obvious choice (in this case, Yard A) but then quickly reverse it (to Yard B) to foil whatever tricks the Tricksters might have planned for him.

And so it was that I arrived at a scientific decision. I chose Yard A, established it as my Decoy Decision, and instantly reversed the deal and threw all my marbles at Yard B.

Pretty clever, huh?

Crouched on the ground below the fence around Yard B, I coiled my legs under me and made a gigantic leap upward, snagged my front paws on the top of the fence, pulled and tugged with my front legs while kicking and scrambling with my hind legs, and finally boosted myself over.

At last, I had reached my destination, and now all that remained was for me to awaken my sister and give her the good news that I had arrived for a visit.

I hated to wake her up. Last time I'd dropped in for a visit, she'd been having trouble with headaches, and I knew that with all the responsibility of raising four pups and so forth, she needed her sleep.

But I didn't want her to think I was an intruder, poking around in the dark. So I went creeping through the yard. Using all my sensory equipment, I managed to locate her darkhouse in the dogness. I could just barely make out the tip-top of the tip of the top of the . . .

I could just barely make out the peak of the roof, let us say, of her doghouse, and on silent paws I slipped across the yard. As I drew closer, I could hear her breathing.

No big shock there. I mean, I had expected to hear her breathing because, well, she was a normal healthy dog and she breathed in her sleep.

But her breathing did seem heavy, and moments later I found out why.

CHAPTER
5

A CASE OF
MISTAKEN IDENTITY

Yes, I was a little surprised that a lady of Maggie's standing in the community would SNORE. I was kind of embarrassed, to tell the truth, that my sister would . . . I mean, we're talking about heavy-duty hog-pen noises.

"Maggie? Oh Maggie. Margaret?" No luck. I had no choice but to raise my voice. "Maggie, I've got a wonderful surprise for you. Uncle Hank is here for a visit! Maggie? HEY!"

That did it, broke the rhythm of her snores. She snorted and grunted, and good heavens, the poor girl must have been having trouble with her sinuses. How could such a sweet fenimum lady make such truck-like noises?

"Maggie, sorry to wake you up, but I just wanted to check in and . . . "

I could see her head now. Big head. Sharp pointed ears. Heavy jowls. Hmmm, she was having a problem with her weight, too.

"Anyway, Mag, it's me again, Hank the Cowdog, and are you my sister Maggie or have I . . . "

A deep voice answered: "Son, my name is Rambo. You have woke me up, and you are fixing to learn what happens to mutts who wake up Great Danes in the middle of the night."

HUH? Great Danes?

Well, we needn't drag this thing out.

On the positive side, I managed to dislodge the foreign object in my throat. On the negative side, what dislodged it was the force of my body being hurled against the fence.

And, yes, I did pick up a few facts about Great Danes. Their "greatness" refers to their size, not to any higher qualities of mind or spirit. And they have no sense of humor at all, I mean, *none.*

Zero.

Zilch.

Never wake up a Great Dane in the middle of the night.

Well, let us say that I had made a slight miscalculation and had entered the wrong yard. Let us say that I was expelled from the yard in a rude manner, and that I was lucky to escape with all four legs attached to their proper places.

That Rambo character was an incredible thug, although if he hadn't caught me by surprise and if I hadn't been handicapped by a foreign object that was hung in my throat, I might have . . .

I might have left the yard anyway, come to think of it.

So there I was, alone again in a dark alley. I didn't dare try another yard-entry at that late hour, for obvious reasons, and so I wandered around for several hours, just killing time.

Not much to report there. I barked at several mutts who barked at me first, and I caught a big black cat picking through the remains of the garbage barrel I had overturned.

In other words, she was stealing MY garbage. But I taught her a valuable lesson about property law. She was crouched there in the alley, see, and thought she was getting by with her sneaky activity, thought that whole alley belonged to her, never saw me creeping up behind her, and . . . heh, heh.

I love doing that to cats. It's one of the things that makes being a dog worthwhile.

If you work it just right, you can creep up on

'em and at the very last second, roar right in their ears. Then, "Reeeeeer! Hiss!" They'll hiss and spit and squawl, turn wrongside out, and run away.

Once in a great while, they'll turn around and pop you on the nose with their claws, as this one did, and sometimes that causes a little blood to flow, but the end result is always worth the sacrifice.

I chased that cat up a utility pole and returned to my garbage barrel and spent the remainder of the night guarding my treasures. I wasn't sure that I needed those treasures but they were by George MINE and I wasn't about to turn them over to a bunch of rinky-dink town cats.

One of the disadvantages of owning treasures is that you have to guard them, and guard duty can be very boring. I remained alert and vigilant until the early morning hours, at which time I probably fell asleep.

Yes, I'm almost sure I fell asleep because the next thing I knew, it was broad daylight and the sun was straight overhead. I leaped up from my bed of grass and papers, shook myself, took a good long stretch, yawned, made a quick inventory of my treasures, and lit out to find my sister's place.

In the light of day, I had no trouble finding it. Yes, it all came back now, all the signs and land-

G.L. Holmes

marks I had missed the night before, how foolish
of me to have missed them, but remember that
the night had been very, very dark.

Extremely dark.

No moon whatsoever.

No dog could have found that yard in the dark.

Okay. Once again, I was faced with a five-foot wooden fence, but once again that was no big deal. I crouched, leaped, hooked front paws, scrambled back legs, and pulled myself up to the summit.

There, balancing myself on the top two-by-four, I pulled myself up to my full height, and cried out in a triumphant voice, "Hey Maggie, surprise! Look who's . . . "

Balancing on a two-by-four is one of the most difficult tricks in the world, especially when you combine it with a triumphant shout, and a lot of times what happens is that a guy will go over the side in a crash-dive situation.

In other words, falling off a fence is no disgrace, even if you happen to swap ends and land on your back.

It was my good fortune to land in a clump of tall dry weeds that softened the blow but also made it very difficult for me to regain my footing.

No problem. All I had to do was kick and scramble . . . but on the other hand, these were large weeds and it appeared that I had gotten myself high-centered in them and, by George, I couldn't get out.

G. L. Holmes

Funny, how those embarrassing moments always seem to come at the worst possible . . . I had wanted to impress my sister with an extra special trick, don't you know, and . . .

Well, there I was, hung up in some derned fool weeds, and here came my nieces and nephews, all four of them, cutest little guys you ever saw.

"It's Uncle Hank!"

"Hi, Uncle Hank!"

I chuckled and looked down at them. They all appeared to be standing upside down because, well, because I was lying on my back in those stupid, idiot weeds.

"Hi kids! Hey, it's great to see you again. Did you see your Uncle Hank balanced up there on that fence, huh? Was that pretty exciting, or what?"

"What are you doing in the weeds, Uncle Hank?"

"Weeds? Oh, you mean these weeds? Just part of the trick, honey, and now I'll just . . . kick my way out of these . . . sometimes it takes a . . . whew, boy, these are some kind of heavy weeds y'all have here!"

"Are you stuck, Uncle Hank?"

"Should we call Momma to help you, Uncle Hank?"

I laughed. "Don't you bother your ma, son, no, I'll just KICK AND STRUGGLE and in no time at all, call your momma, son, I think I'm hung up."

The boy — Roscoe, I think it was — went scampering over to the doghouse. "Momma, Momma, come quick! Uncle Hank's here!"

"Oh good heavens! He couldn't have come at a . . . "

"Come quick! He fell in some weeds and can't get out."

I couldn't make out what she said then, but I could tell, just by the tone of her voice, that she was pretty concerned about me.

Good old Mag! She had some peculiar ways and over the years we hadn't seen eye-to-eye on everything, but when it came down to taking care of her kinfolks, hey, she was solid as a rock.

She followed Roscoe over to the clump of weeds. She seemed to be wearing a peculiar smile, almost a smirk, although it was hard to tell since I was looking at her upside down.

"Good heavens, Henry, what are you doing!"

"Hi, Mag, fine thanks, great to see you again. Oh, I took a little tumble off the fence, you might say, and by George, I seem to be hung up in these weeds."

"Yes, so it seems, Henry. And what were you doing on top of the fence?"

"Oh, just goofing around, Mag. You know me. Heck, I wanted to give these kids a little . . . tell you what, Mag, why don't we talk about it after you help me get out of here?"

She came over and pushed down on the weeds

with her front paws. It didn't take much to get me out of there, just a little shove on the weeds, and bingo, I was out of that mess and back on the ground.

I gave myself a good shake and knocked off some of those weed stems, kind of spruced myself up because, hey, I wasn't slumming any more. I was visiting my sister!

Well, naturally, all four kids came rushing up to me.

"Hi, Uncle Hank!"

"Do another trick for us, Uncle Hank!"

"Yeah, and tell us a story about coyotes and wolfs!"

I looked down at them and smiled. "All in good time, kids, all in good time. But first, let me say hello to my favorite sister." I walked over to her and gave her a hug. "Maggie! It's great to see you again."

She embraced me but then pulled away. She lifted her nose and sniffed the air. "Henry, I think I smell . . . garbage."

"Garbage? Hmmm. That's odd. Oh, I know what it is. There's garbage strewn all over the alley, Mag, terrible sight. Do you have cats in this neighborhood?"

"Well . . . yes, but . . . "

"There you are! I knew it. Those cats have

been picking around in the garbage barrels. In fact, I caught one in the act and ran her up a pole. To be honest about it, Maggie, I was shocked to see your alley in such a mess."

"Oh. Well, of course, we try to . . . "

"Don't worry about it, Maggie. I know it's not your fault, but it was a little shocking. And, who knows, I might have picked up some of that garbage smell just walking down the alley, is probably what happened."

"I'm sure that's what it was, Henry."

Heh, heh. Dodged a bullet there.

"Perhaps," she added with a smile, "you'll have to be more careful *when you leave*. I wouldn't want you *going back to the ranch* smelling of garbage. I know how fussy you are about those things."

Little Spot, the other boy, pushed his way into the conversation. "You're not leaving, are you, Uncle Hank? Can't you stay a while and tell us a story?"

For some reason, Maggie's eyes grew as wide as plates. "Hush, child! Your uncle is a very busy dog."

I chuckled "That's okay, Mag. He's right. By George, when you get too busy to visit your kinfolks, you're just too busy."

"Uh, yes, but Henry, we know you have a ranch

to take care of, and we understand that you're anxious to get back to your work."

"Well, yes, I am a pretty busy dog. I mean, running that ranch all by myself is no small potatoes."

She seemed to be edging towards the fence. "Certainly not! I don't know how you do it."

"It's tough, Mag. A lot of dogs couldn't handle it."

By this time we had reached the fence. Maggie smiled and turned her adoring eyes on me. "Well, Henry, this is goodbye. Do come again sometime when we're all not so busy."

"Yes, I sure will, Mag."

I was about to kiss them all goodbye when all of a sudden, I noticed something that changed my plans entirely.

CHAPTER
6

MAGGIE HAS
A FAINTING SPELL

I heard Maggie say, "We're so glad you dropped by to say hello before you had to say
goodbye."

But I heardly hard her words, hardly heard her
words, because by then I had begun to notice
the sad faces of my nieces and nephews. It really
touched my heart to see them looking that way.

"Hey, kids, what's with the long faces and the
pooched-out lips?"

It was Roscoe who spoke. "We wanted to hear
a story, Uncle Hank. Couldn't you tell us just one
before you leave?"

I heaved a sigh and turned to my sister. "What
do you think, Maggie? Should I stick around just
long enough to tell 'em one little story?"

The kids sent up a cheer. And Maggie? Well, she was just beside herself.

A guy tends to forget how much these little visits mean to the kinfolks, especially the ladies.

I went trooping over to the doghouse, with all four pups scampering along behind me, and flopped down on a nice clean piece of carpet. The pups gathered around in front of me.

I started off by telling them the story of how I single-handedly whipped the entire Coyote Nation and won the heart of Missy Coyote, the lovely coyote princess.

The boys loved the part about the fighting, how I whipped Rip and Snort and Scraunch in deadly hand-to-hand combat. And the gals, well, they wanted to know every little detail about Missy.

"Was she pretty, Uncle Hank?"

"Pretty? Honey, to this very day, I dream about her and often regret that I didn't become a cannibal. Say, did I ever tell you boys what the coyote warriors do to impress their girlfriends? They find a dead skunk, see, and . . . "

Maggie had been hovering nearby, but now she came swooping in. "Children, we need to clean up around the house. You can pick up your things and listen to your uncle at the same time. That won't bother you, will it, Henry?"

"Oh, that's fine, Mag. I can talk while they work. Anyway, kids, what these wild coyote warriors do when they really want to impress their lady friends is, they find 'em a dead skunk, see, and . . . "

All at once the air seemed to be filled with dust — so much that I could hardly breathe. It caused me to sneeze, in fact. I glanced around and . . . oh, Maggie had taken a rug in her teeth and was giving it a good shake.

She hadn't noticed that she was doing this directly upwind from me. I moved to get out of the dust cloud and went on with my story.

"Anyways, these coyote warriors, when they really want to make an impression on the gals, they . . . "

Cough, wheeze!

She was shaking it again, and believe it or not, the wind had shifted so that it carried the dust right into my face!

I moved again. "As I was saying, kids, these tough old coyote wariors . . . "

More dust. Well, I had a heck of a time finishing my story, but I'm no quitter and I got 'er done. By that time the kids were so caught up in storytelling that they begged — and we're talking about INSISTED and DEMANDED — that I tell another one.

So, what the heck, I launched into one about

the time I saved the lovely Miss Beulah from a
villain named Rufus.

It was then that, suddenly, without any warning
whatever, my sister swooned and fell over on
the ground.

Had an attack of something.

Fainted.

Well, you know me. I rushed to her side. "Maggie, speak to me! What's happened to you?"

"Ohhhh, it's these spells again, Henry."

"Holy smokes, you had one of these attacks the last time I was here."

"Yes, I know."

"Is the old head hurting you again?"

"Ohhh, terrible headache!"

"And probably an upset stomach to go along with it?"

"Ohhh, terrible upset stomach!"

"And how about dizziness? Are you experiencing any dizziness?"

"Ohhh, terrible dizziness!"

"It must be all this dust, Maggie. It was starting to bother me too."

Her voice was very weak and trembly. "No, not the dust. The spells seem to be triggered by nerves. Tension."

"Nerves, tension, yes, I get the picture."

"And too much company."

"Okay, yes, I'm beginning to see a pattern here." I turned to the pups. "Kids, your mother's headaches are brought on my nerves and tension and tensionous nerves. I'm putting her to bed for the rest of the day."

"Yes," she moaned, "and no company."

"Right. I was getting to that." I turned back to the kids. "If anybody shows up around here, tell 'em your ma is sick in bed and can't be bothered."

"Thank you, Henry. You've been so kind."

"No problem, glad to do it."

"And do come back some other time."

"Hey, I'll do better than that."

"Goodbye, Henry."

"I'm staying until you get back on your feet."

"Ohhhhhh!"

"Is it getting worse, Mag?"

"It's getting REAL."

"Yes, and that's the worst kind. Real pain is really painful."

She struggled to her feet and looked at me with . . . hummm, that was a pretty ferocious look she pointed at me, although I sure understood how those headaches could put you in a bad mood.

"Here, Mag, let me help you."

"Haven't you done enough already?"

"Hey, it was nothing, really."

"You'll regret this, Henry."

"Not at all, Sis. It's the least I could do." She staggered into the doghouse. "And don't worry about the kids. Uncle Hank is in charge of everything."

"Ohhhhhh!"

When she was gone, I turned to the pups. "I'm sure worried about your ma. Does she have these spells often?"

"Only once before," said April. "The last time you were here."

"Boy, that's a piece of good luck. I mean, if she's going to have spells, better that she has them when I'm around to help."

"The last time, she said she had bad allergies to certain characters."

"Yes, those allergies can cause a lot of misery. Well, kids, what should we do now? You want to have some more storytime? Take a nap? Dig a hole? What do you think?"

Little Roscoe held up his paw. "Last time, you took us on a garbage patrol. Boy, that was fun!"

"Yes, I remember it well, and by George, if that's what . . . "

BAM, BAM, BAM!

Someone or something was banging on the front gate. Little Barbara went scampering over to answer it. I reminded her that Maggie was too sick to be bothered with company.

When she came back, I knew something was wrong. Her eyes were big and she looked scared.

"Uncle Hank, it's the dog next door. He wants to see Mother."

"Well, that's too bad. He can't. You go back

and tell him that your Uncle Hank told him to go chase his tail."

Spot spoke up then. "Be careful, Uncle Hank. He's BIG and he's MEAN!"

I chuckled at that. "Son, I've already told you what I do to the cannibals out at the ranch. Big and mean is nothing new to me."

"Yeah, but he's REAL big and mean. And he's a bully. He comes into our yard and steals our bones."

That got my attention. "Oh yeah? Steals bones from my nieces and nephews?"

"And our dog food too."

"Huh. What does your ma think of this?"

Roscoe pushed forward. "She hates him but she's scared of him. He says he'll beat us all up if we don't give him what he wants."

By that time I was on my feet, limbering up my shoulder muscles. "You know, kids, I haven't met this guy, but already I have a feeling that I'm not going to like him."

"You'll hate him too, Uncle Hank," said Barbara. "He barks at cars all the time."

"Yeah," said April, "and he's beat up every dog in the neighborhood, and he steals and cheats and talks naughty"

"Talks naughty, huh? Not in front of you kids, I hope." They nodded their heads, all four of them. "Well, that settles it. Any dog that steals bones and talks naughty in front of my little kin-folks is looking for trouble. And kids," I gave them a wink, "I think he came to the right place to find it."

They clapped their paws and cheered. "Yea Uncle Hank!"

With their cheering and applause ringing in my ears, I swaggered over to the gate and prepared to clean house on the neighborhood thug.

C H A P T E R
7

UH OH

I marched up to the gate. I could hear heavy
breathing on the other side, which gave me
my first clue in the case: the neighborhood thug
had sinus trouble. I salted that information away
for future use.

"You are hearing the voice of Hank the Cowdog, Head of Ranch Security. This yard is closed
to traffic for the rest of the afternoon. My sister
has been put to bed due to health problems. We
appreciate your concern, and goodbye."

Heavy breathing.

"In other words, go away."

More heavy breathing.

"Hey buddy, you'll never sneak up on anyone
with that sinus problem. Your breathing sounds

like a diesel truck. In other words, I know you're still there."

Heavier breathing.

"See? I told you you were still there. You can't fool me. Well, go ahead and breathe all you want, it's a free country, but you absolutely are not coming into this yard."

Still heavier breathing.

I turned back to the kids and gave 'em a wink. "And let me tell you something else, pal. The next time you get the urge to steal a bone, I'd advise you to try some other yard, because this yard is now under the jurisdiction of Hank..."

BAM!

All at once the gate flew open and I found myself more or less smashed between the gate and the fence. When the stars and checkers cleared from my head, I looked up and ... HUH? My goodness, that was a pretty big dog.

Real big dog.

A small horse?

Looked a whole lot like a Great Dane.

Had I met this guy before?

Uh oh.

Rambo.

The pups ran for cover when he came bursting through the gate. I didn't, for obvious reasons. He ran his eyes over the yard, and then he spoke

in a voice that matched up with the heavy breathing I had noted before. A big, heavy voice, in other words.

"Where is this loud-mouthed cowdog?"

I stood perfectly still against the fence, hoping that he might think I was a shrub or something. You never know. But he didn't. His huge, ugly, bloodshot eyes swung around and locked on me.

"What are you doing back there?"

"Me?"

"Yeah, you. I ain't talking to the gate."

"I knew that. You struck me as the kind of dog who wouldn't go around talking to gates."

"Answer the question."

"Okay, fine, sure. That's easy enough. What am I doing back here?"

"Yeah? That's the question. What's the answer?"

"Oh, you wanted the answer?" I laughed. "I thought you wanted to hear the question again." I laughed. "I'm a little heard of harding."

"What?"

"I said, I'm a little hard of hearing."

"Oh. Too bad."

"What?"

"I said, too bad!"

"Well, two's better than one."

He lumbered over to me and popped me on the chin so that my jaws snapped shut. "You know what? I don't like your looks and I don't like dogs who don't listen when I talk. Maybe you'd like to start listening better."

"I was about to suggest that."

"Good. Do you know who I am?"

"Uh, let's see. Your name wouldn't be Trigger, would it?" He popped me on the chin again. "Or Rambo, how about Rambo?"

He gave me a smirk. "Now you've got it. I'm Rambo and I own this town."

"It's a great little town, I've always liked it."

"Good for you. Where's the cowdog?"

I found myself coughing. "Cowdog? Whatever made you think there might be a cowdog around here?"

He brought his nose right up to my face. "You know what I think? I think you look like a cowdog."

"Me, a cowdog? Ha, ha, ha. Oh no, not me. I'm a hogdog, Harry the Hogdog. There's a huge difference between hogdogs and cowdogs."

"Oh yeah? Like what?"

"Well, you have your hogs and you have your cows, and they're very different. Your, uh, hogs say 'Oink,' and your cows say 'Moo,' and that's a pretty huge difference right there. No hog has ever said 'Moo.'"

He popped my chin again.

"Except on very rare occasions, that is."

He did it again.

"You keep popping me on the chin."

"You keep talking stupid. Do I need you to tell me that no hog has ever said 'Moo?'"

"Maybe not." He popped me again. "In other words, NO."

"That's better. Now, tell me something else."

"Sure, anything at all, just ask."

He leaned forward and drilled me with those ugly eyes. "Have we met before?"

All at once I had trouble breathing. "You know, I was just asking myself that same question, and the answer is no. No, we haven't met before. Never. Never ever. Honest."

"Your face looks familiar."

"You won't believe this, but I hear that all the time. Almost every day some dog comes up to me and says, 'Your face looks familiar to me.' I've just got a familiar face, that's all."

"I think we've met. It was in the middle of the night."

"No, wrong dog. I was out of town that night."

"Which night?"

"The, uh, night we didn't meet in the middle of the night. I was gone. Out of town. Miles away. No kidding."

"I think we've met, and . . . " All at once his ears shot up and he turned his head towards the street. "I hear a car coming. Stay right where you are. Don't move a hair."

And with that, he loped out the gate and began barking at a car in the street.

While he was gone, I concentrated hard on

not moving a hair. It wasn't as simple as you might suppose. I have many hairs on my body and they're all easily moved.

I was standing there against the fence when I heard the voice of Little Roscoe. He came creeping out from behind a lawn chair. "Uncle Hank? Did you run him off?"

"Not yet, son, we're, uh, still negotiating a few points. This may take a little longer than I thought."

"Are you going to beat him up, like you said?"

I laughed. "Ha, ha, ha. You know, son, nothing in this old world is more violent than violence, and violence is a terrible thing."

"Yeah, but you sure used it on those coyotes, didn't you?"

"Son, it's possible that you misquoted me. I've always favored the path of reason and compromise."

"You mean you're scared?"

"I, uh, I'm finding more and more things to admire about Mister Rambo as we, uh, continue our ... you'd better hide, son, he's coming back."

Rambo returned to the yard in that long trot of his. He had a big smile plastered across his jowels. "Did you see me bark at that car?"

"Oh yes, very impressive, I've never ... "

CLUNK!

He bopped me on the chin again. "Then you moved a hair. When I tell you not to move a hair, Harry, I mean don't move a hair. You got that?"

"Yes. Sir. Yes sir, sir."

"But it was impressive, wasn't it? I love barking at cars. It's my passion. It's my vice. It's my greatest strength and my greatest weakness." He stuck his nose right in my face. "I'm a Car-Barkaholic, did you know that?"

"I didn't know that."

"I can't leave 'em alone. Every time I see a car coming down the street, I get this terrible urge to tear off his wheels and eat his doors." He threw a glance to the left. "Where's Maggie?"

"She's, uh, sick. Ill. Unable to speak or walk. We think she's come down with Terminal Rutabaga."

"I never heard of it."

"That's because everyone who's ever heard of it has died a miserable death. It's that contagious. If I were you, I'd leave right now."

"You would, huh? If Maggie's so sick, how come she just came out of her doghouse?"

I glanced over in that direction and, sure enough, she had just stepped out. "I think I can explain everything if you . . . "

"Shat up. And don't move a hair until I tell you." He left me there against the fence and swaggered over in Maggie's direction.

When she saw him, her face showed fear, then anger. "So it's you again. You're back."

"Yeah, I'm back. I want your bones. I want your dog food. And I want a big kiss, Maggie."

She stomped over to him, drew back her paw, and whacked him across the face. "There's the only kiss you'll get from me, you heartless bully!"

An ugly laugh came boiling out of his throat. "That's no way to treat the best car-barking dog in Texas. I was expecting something better."

"All right, then here's something better." She drew back and hit him another lick, this one even harder than the first one. And it had just about the same effect. Nothing.

With one rapid motion, Rambo threw her to the ground and held her down with one paw. "You'll stay on the ground, Maggie, until you're ready to give me a kiss."

At that point I stepped out of the shadows and faced him. "Hey Rambo, I'm Hank the Cowdog and that's my sister. Get out of the yard while you still have four legs to carry you."

CHAPTER 8

A TERRIBLE FIGHT

All at once the pups appeared from behind bushes and lawn chairs and raised a cheer. I needed a cheer because my legs were shaking so badly I could hardly stand up.

"Yea Uncle Hank! That's telling him! Go get him, Uncle Hank! Beat him up!"

Rambo's gaze drifted from me to the kids and back to me. A sneer wiggled across his mouth and he nodded his head. "I remember now. You're the jerk that woke me up in the middle of the night."

"That's ram, Rightbo, and I'm the jerk that's fixing to wake you up again."

He laughed. "Say, pooch, do you remember what happened to you last night?"

"Sure. You landed one lucky punch. So what?"

"I swept my yard with your carcass and then I threw you against the fence, and then I threw you OVER the fence, is what I did."

"That's right, one lucky punch, but you won't be so lucky this time, Rambo. Now, for the last time, get your paws off my sister and get out of this yard."

He laid his ears flat against his head and leaned his ugly face in my direction. "Make me."

"One more smart remark like that, Rambo, and I'll be forced to make you."

"Make me."

"Keep saying that, Rambo, and just see what happens."

I was stalling for time, see, because I wasn't optimistic about my chances of making that monster-dog do anything. We stood there glaring each other, when all at once Roscoe marched up beside me.

"Come on, Uncle Hank, I'll help you. We're cowdogs and we're not scared of any old Great Dane, are we, Uncle Hank?"

You know, up to that moment I had been, well, not exactly scared but . . . a little uneasy, let us say. Nervous. Anxious. A wee bit unsure of myself. But when I looked down at that little cowdog pup and saw that determined gleam in his eyes, hey, all at once I remembered who I was and where I'd come from.

Yes, we were cowdogs, and that was something special. I took a step towards the bully. "This could be your last chance, Rambo. Leave the yard and we'll forget the whole thing."

He was grinning. "And if I don't? What'll we do then, Mister Cowdog?" He looked down at my sister. "Come on, Maggie, give me one little kiss before I take care of your brother."

"Don't touch me, let me up this very minute, and don't you dare lay a paw on Henry, or so help me I'll . . . "

"Har, har, har! This is almost as much fun as barking at cars." His eyes drifted up to me. "What are you going to do now, cowdog? The suspension is killing me."

Roscoe was jumping up and down. "Let's jump him, Uncle Hank! I'll be right beside you."

Spot came up and joined us. "Yeah, and me too."

"Well, by George, we've got him outnumbered. All right, guys, take the first leg you come to and start chewing. Let's wade in and see what we can do. Charge, attack, bonzai!"

I led the charge and delivered a piledriver blow to Rambo's chest. Imagine, if you will, a piledriver smashing into the side of a mountain of solid granite. That will give you some idea of the damage I inflicted. Not much. In fact, there for a moment or two, we thought we might need to bring up a new piledriver.

You see, the mountain was not only big and solid, but it also struck back, which sort of scattered our piledriver over half an acre before we could put everything back together and throw it back into action.

Even though I got myself, uh, diverted there for a minute or two, the boys came in the second wave and started chewing on Rambo's legs. By that time April and Barbara had come out of hiding and decided to join the crusade, and they came in the third wave. It happened that Rambo had two more legs to chew, and that's where they went.

Then Maggie got herself out from under Rambo's paw, and she jumped up and made the fourth wave. There were many things she had never learned about yard fighting, but she was aroused enough to be about half-dangerous. She chewed for a while and then she hit for a while, and then she went back to chewing.

I think Mister Rambo was a little surprised by this show of family unity. Those kids weren't big enough to knock down a fly, but they had sharp

little teeth and they were about to eat his legs
off. He'd shake one off, but the other three went
right on chewing.

And he was so preoccupied with saving his
legs that I was able to mount a second attack. I
landed a dandy left hook under his chin. What
it did to his chin I can't say, but it liked to have
broke my paw in half. Then I jumped on his back
and began gnawing on his ears.

He didn't like that! No siree, and that's probably why he bucked so hard and pitched me into the barbecue pit. Well, I didn't let a little thing like that slow me down. In a flash, I was back in the middle of things.

I landed a left to his nose, a right to his chin (ouch!), and another left to his nose. I didn't want to think about what he might have done to me if Maggie and the kids hadn't been there, but I didn't have to think about it, because they were.

Old Rambo was a slow learner, but after several minutes he began to realize that he was coming out on the short end of this deal. He started

G.L. Holmes

edging towards the gate, which was pretty interesting to watch since he had a biting pup attached to all four legs and an angry mother barking in his ear.

At last he jumped into the air and kicked his legs, and pups went rolling in all directions. Then he made a run for the gate. When he got there, he stopped and turned back to us. His eyes were seething with cold hatred and fury.

"Okay, you win this round, but you'll live to regret it. I'll be back. You won't know when I'm coming. It might be in the dark of night or the light of day, but I'll be back. Don't leave the yard. Don't sleep. Don't get careless, 'cause if you do, I'LL GET YOU! And cowdog, you'll be the first to go."

And with that, he whirled around and left in a lope.

I went to the gate and eased it shut with my nose. Closing the gate was more of a formality than anything else. Rambo had already proved that he could jump up on the other side and pop the latching mechanism any time he wanted. But still, I felt better with the gate shut.

By this time the kids were cheering and jumping around.

"We did it! We whipped the bully!"

"Yeah, we showed him!"

"Hooray for Uncle Hank! Hooray for the family!"

It was a joyous occasion, a moment of triumph in the life of a cowdog family. We had worked together and we had won. It seemed a pretty good time to celebrate our victory with a song, and I happened to know one that was just right for the occasion. Here's how it went.

Hymn To The Home

Bless our family, bless our love,
Make it shine like stars above.

Bless our parents, keep them strong,
Let them teach us right from wrong.

Bless these children, help them learn
Patience, virtue, and concern.

Bless this home and bless us all,
Bless this roof and bless these walls.

Bless the food our bodies need,
Bless the hands that us do feed.

Bless our voices, bless our song,
Harmony will make us strong.

Yes sir, it was a great occasion. I turned to Maggie and gave her a wink. "Nice work, Sis. All these years I never knew you had such a talent for alley fighting. By George, you gave old Rambo's ears quite a chewing."

"Thank you, Henry, and I must admit that your rough cowdog ways came in handy. I don't know what we would have done without you." She leaned forward and, you won't believe this, kissed me on the cheek. Then she coughed. "But I wish we could do something about that odor."

The kids raised a cheer. "Hooray for Mom! Hooray for Uncle Hank! Hooray for the Cowdog Kids!"

Our celebration lasted all afternoon. We played Chase The Sock, Hide the Tennis Shoe, Tug the Bone, and Free For All Against Uncle Hank. Outside the yard, we could hear the neighborhood thug barking at cars, but he didn't bother us.

He wouldn't have dared bother us. I mean, we had taught that guy a lesson he wouldn't forget.

By George, it was a dandy picnic, and the next thing we knew, it was dark. The pups and I went trooping up to the doghouse, where Maggie had spent the afternoon sunning herself and watching us romp and play. She scolded the pups for getting themselves all covered with dust and grass, but she knew they'd had a good, wholesome afternoon and she didn't get too serious about the scolding.

Say, all that romping around with the kids had just about wore me out and I was ready to do some serious sleeping. I found myself a nice comfortable spot in front of the doghouse, scratched around on it, turned three circles, and collapsed.

The pups followed my example, and before long, all four of them were curled up beside me and we were throwing up long lines of Zs. It was the perfect way to end a perfect day.

I was in the midst of a wonderful dream about Miss Beulah the Collie when I heard someone calling my name.

"Henry?"

"Uh mug womp snork snicklefritz."

"Henry, wake up. I hear something."

I sat up and studied the dark face before me. "What do you mean, you murgled the skiffering porkchop heard something?"

"Henry, I don't want to alarm you, but *someone is lurking over by the fence*!!"

THE FORT
IS SURROUNDED

It was Maggie, and there was an edge of fear in her voice. It was nice that she didn't want to alarm me, but she did anyway.

I leaped to my feet and stepped on a pup or two before I could get my bearings.

"I'm sorry to wake you up," she whispered.

"Oh, no problem, I wasn't asnork, just resting my porkchops."

"Follow me."

She went creeping across the yard, and as we approached the south fence, I began picking up the sound myself. It was faint at first, but it grew louder as we approached the fence.

It was a very spooky sound, and I'll admit that it raised a strip of hair two inches wide all the way from the back of my neck to the tip of my tail.

Someone was on the other side of the fence . . . BREATHING!!

Breathing is normal, right? Everybody does it several times a day and it's nothing to get excited about, right? I agree with the theory, but let me tell you something. When you wake up from a deep sleep and hear HEAVY BREATHING on the other side of the fence, in the dark of night . . . fellers, that's about the spookiest sound in the whole entire world.

Especially if you have reason to suspect that the heavy breather happens to be a huge monster Great Dane dog who's doctoring a grudge.

Nursing a grudge.

Holding a grudge.

. . . a monster Great Dane who's holding a grudge and thinking wicked thoughts and plotting revenge in the deep dead dark of the night.

And take my word for it, that's scary.

You know, I don't enjoy being scared, especially of something I can't see. I'd rather get the thing out into the open and fight it, even if I get whipped in the process.

"All right, Rambo, we know you're there. Are you ready for Round Two?" No answer. "You're not fooling anybody, and furthermore, we're not the least bit scared." Still no answer. "Come on over the fence, Rambo, and we'll see what you're made of."

Nothing but heavy breathing.

I gave Maggie the sign and we moved to another part of the yard where we could talk. She looked worried. I expect that I did too, because I was.

"Henry, I'm frightened. What should we do about this?"

"Funny that you should ask, Mag. I was just wondering the same thing."

"It's obvious that he's chosen to torment us, to make us live in a state of constant fear."

"Yes, that guy is smarter and deviouser than I ever supposed. This could go on for weeks."

"How long did you plan to stay, Henry?"

"Not for weeks."

"Oh dear."

I began pacing. My mind seems to work better when I pace, don't you see. "Maggie, he's got us over a bucket. We're trapped in our own yard. All we can do is sit in here like a bunch of rabbits and wait for him to make the next move."

"Maybe we could post a guard."

"Yes, we could post a guard, but what if he decides to drag it out for days or weeks? Time is on his side. All he has to do is wait. By the time he decides to make his move, we'll be worn out from worry and lack of sleep. We'll be fighting amongst ourselves. We'll lose our spirit of teamwork. That's his strategy, Maggie, divide and conquer."

"Oh, he's such a hateful dog! Why did he have to live next door to us?" She heaved a sigh and was quiet for a moment. "Henry, it's hopeless, I can see that now. I should have given him his stupid kiss and let him take the childrens' bones."

"No, Mag. Once you cave in to a bully, there's no end to it."

"Well? He's going to win anyway, and the longer we put it off, the worse it's going to be." She stood up. "I'll go tell him that we surrender."

"Whoa, hold on, wait a minute, halt. Hey Maggie, you left the ranch many years ago but you're still a cowdog, and cowdogs don't surrender."

"That's easy for you to say, Henry. You can leave and go back to your ranch, but we have to stay here. I must think of the children."

"Yeah, well, I'm thinking of the children too. I don't want 'em to grow up cowards, afraid of every bully who happens to be bigger and louder than they are. There's a very important principle involved here."

"Henry, you're right but you're wrong."

"No, I'm right but I'm right. Before I'd let you

surrender to that jerk, I'd go over that fence and challenge him to a fight to the death."

"And then where would we be? Getting yourself killed in battle might solve YOUR problem, but it wouldn't solve mine or the childrens'. No, Henry, there's no other way."

"Mag, I can't stand by and watch you do this. It goes against everything I've ever believed in."

"Then you should go, Henry. Thank you for trying. I wish it had worked out better." She started towards the fence but stopped and came back a few steps. "Henry, I really was proud of you today. Just for a few hours, you made us feel like real cowdogs. Goodbye."

"Goodbye, Maggie, and good luck."

She went to the south fence and I went to the back of the yard. As I crouched down and prepared to spring up on the fence, I heard a burst of wicked laughter. Then:

"That's fine, Maggie, that's real fine. But what does your bumpkin brother think about it?"

"Oh," she said in a sad voice, "he left hours ago."

"Har, har, har! I knew he was yellow. I just wish I could have had one more chance to sweep the yard with him."

All my muscles froze. I listened to the pounding

of my heart. I couldn't stand the thought of running away with my tail between my legs, leaving my sister to be bullied and terrorized by that hoodlum dog.

I whirled around and started toward the sound of his voice. But then I remembered: Maggie had asked me to leave. She had made her choice, and it didn't include me.

Before I could think about it any more, I ran straight for the back fence, leaped high in the air, climbed over the top, hit the ground, and ran south down the alley as hard as I could run.

Yes, I was running away from everything I believed in. I was running away from myself, my pride, my past, my cowdog heritage, everything that mattered. And what really made me sick was that *one part of me was glad to be running away*!

But I couldn't silence that still, small voice inside my head: "Rambo said you were yellow, Hank, and sure enough, you are. Look at you! You're leaving your sister and her kids to a bully. Never mind what Maggie said. YOU knew what needed to be done and you didn't do it. You chose to run and to forget, but you can't forget. 'A cowdog never surrenders,' Hank old boy, but you surrendered."

I gritted my teeth and ran harder than ever. I

had to get away from there! I had to get out of town, away from that voice inside my head.

I sprinted down the alley, tripping over weeds and clods of hardened mud. I couldn't see where I was going but I didn't care. I had to get out of town.

Somewhere near the south edge of town, I saw a big yellow tomcat sitting in the moonlight. He was just sitting there in the middle of the alley, minding his own business and licking his front paw.

Well, maybe I couldn't whip Rambo but I could sure as thunder beat up a cat and make him the whipping post for all my scapegoats. My anger and frustration came to a point and focused on that cat. I increased speed, took dead aim at him, and . . .

Most cats will run from a dog, but every once in a great while we find one that will stand his ground and fight. Your tomcats seem to be more prone to that sort of irrational behavior than others, and yes, once in a great while . . .

As I say, he was a big cat, and the closer I came to him the bigger he looked. I kept waiting for him to hiss and run. By the time I began to suspect that he might NOT run, it was too late to alter course.

Yikes!

Yes, he slapped me across the nose with a handful of very sharp claws, and yes, he somehow managed to climb upon my back, and no, I don't suppose we need to discuss it any more.

What really matters is that I finally bucked him off and escaped with some excellent research material on the nature of tomcats.

By the time I had shed that insane tomcat, I had reached the south edge of town. Up ahead, I could see one last mercury-vapor yard light, and beyond that, nothing but darkness and open prairie.

I ran towards the light and began to realize that I was approaching the Devil's Island For Dogs — the Twitchell Dog Pound. That was no place for me, so I . . . on the other hand, I knew a guy who lived there, or did at one time.

G.L.Holmes

His name was Ralph, Dog-Pound Ralph. Not a bad guy, if you you could tolerate his slow manner and his dreary basset-hound face.

And it suddenly occurred to me that Dog-Pound Ralph might have a role to play in a plan that had just taken shape in my mind — a plan that just might provide a solution to the Rambo Problem.

C H A P T E R
10

DOG-POUND RALPH

I slowed to a walk and studied the situation up ahead. I didn't suppose that the dog-catcher would be at the pound at that hour of the night, but I didn't care to take any chances.

If I had seen his white pickup with the cage in the back, I wouldn't have risked a visit with Ralph. He was a nice guy and all that, but there were many nice guys in this world, and the nicest of them didn't hang out with dogcatchers.

I checked out the place, gave it a thorough going-over with my optical scanners, and came up with no signs of the dogcatcher. At that point, I began to relax and resumed my journey.

The dog pound had always struck me as kind of a lonesome place, sitting up there on that little hill with no trees anywhere around and with the

wind moaning through the mesh of the pens. Why Ralph chose to stay there was a mystery to me. I would have found it depressing.

Well, I marched up to Cell Number 3, which is where Ralph had stayed last time I'd visited. Sure enough, there he was, stretched out on an old carpet sample that lay on the cement floor. I pushed open the nose with my door and went inside.

He appeared to be dead asleep, with one paw in the water bowl. I sat down for a moment to rest and gather up my reserves of energy.

"Ralph? Wake up, Ralph. An old and dear friend has dropped in for a visit."

"Skaw, scruff, snort, zzzzz. Can't swim, zzzzz."

"You must be dreaming."

"Drowning!"

"No, dreaming."

"Help!"

"Ralph, are you awake?"

"No, but I'm fixing to drown!"

"That's absurd. Oh, I see. Your paw is in the water bowl, which is sending confusing signals to your sleeping mind. Remove your paw from the water."

He rolled over and stared at me. His ears were crooked and so were his eyes. "Did you say that my pa's in the water and he's fixing to drown?"

I smiled. "You just removed it, Ralph. All's well."

"Were you just talking about my pa?"

"Yes, your paw was in the water."

"What about Ma?"

I narrowed my eyes at him. "Ralph, you have trouble waking up, don't you?"

"Uh huh. I sure hope he got out."

"Who?"

"My pa. He never could swim a lick."

"Oh, I see now. You thought I said pa, when actually I said paw." I paced away from him. "Ralph, this is your lucky day."

"Thanks, but it looks like night to me."

"That's true, but not for long. Day follows night."

"Not if you sleep all the time, it don't."

"Ralph, I'm sure you remember me." I waited. He yawned. "I say, I'm sure you remember me."

"Oh sure. You're Clyde."

"Uh, no, not Clyde."

"Harvey?"

"No."

"Spot?"

I chuckled. "You're still asleep, Ralph, which explains why you don't recognize me. Walk around, give yourself a nice stretch, and it'll all come back to you."

He rolled out of bed, jacked himself up to a standing position, and gave his head a shake. Those big ears popped like a bullwhip.

"Oh yeah," he said, after a yawn, "now I remember."

"I thought you would."

"You served time here once, didn't you?"

"That's correct, Ralph. I had been arrested on suspicion of hydrophobia."

"Uh huh, yup, it's all coming back now."

"It was a pretty scary experience, actually, and I came within a whisker of getting my head chopped off and sent to the state lab in Houston."

"Austin. State lab's in Austin. Uh huh, it's coming back now."

"I thought it would. A guy doesn't forget the dogs he served time with on Death Row. It's a very intense kind of experience."

"Uh huh." He walked around in a circle, then went to the water bowl and took a drink. His toenails clicked on the cement when he walked. "Yup, I've got you pegged now. Your name's Oscar. It took me a minute."

I narrowed my eyes and glared at him. "Ralph, your memory's not so good. Not only am I not Oscar, I don't even know a dog named Oscar."

"Huh. I sure struck out on the names. What day is this?"

"Monday. Thursday. What's time to a dog, Ralph?"

He sat down and began scratching his ear. "Just thought I'd ask. Your name wouldn't be Rocky, would it?"

"No, it wouldn't be, and come to think of it, I'm sorry that I went to the trouble to come by and say hello. My name, for your information, is

Hank the Cowdog. And I happen to be Head of Ranch Security on a place south of town."

"Huh."

"It's a big outfit, huge outfit. I'm sure you've heard of the Four Sixes Ranch, the Pitchfork, and the JA?"

"Not really."

"Well, my outfit is bigger than all those put together."

"I'll be derned."

"And I'm Head of Ranch Security."

"Oh yeah, I thought maybe that was you."

"Thanks, Ralph, but I'm afraid that won't make up for the damage you've already done. I can see that I'm not welcome here, and it just so happens that I have many warm and loyal friends in this town and I think it's time for me to leave."

I got up to leave but didn't walk very fast.

"Oh, don't be that way. You walked in here and woke me up, and I'm a little slow on the gitty-up. I guess I've been asleep for three days straight."

"Asleep for three days! Don't you ever do anything around here besides sleep?"

He yawned. "Oh, yeah. Sometimes I get me a drink of water, and every once in a while I'll eat a bite."

"You must be bored out of your mind. Don't you ever wish you could do something?"

"Like what?"

"Well, I don't know. Play ball?"

"Hurts my teeth."

"Chase cats? Hunt rabbits?"

He stared at me with those mournful basset eyes. "You know, I chased a cat once, but it took so much energy, I never did it again. I guess you could say that I don't have a whole mountain of ambition."

I began pacing back and forth in front of him. "Yes, and that's too bad, Ralph. I mean, in many ways you're not such a bad guy."

"Thanks."

"But here you are, lolling around and sleeping in the middle of the night, doing nothing with your life, wasting your talents in a two-bit jailhouse, and while you're doing nothing, Life goes right on without you."

"I was afraid of that."

"Ralph, it breaks my heart to see you like this — too lazy even to remember the name of a friend!"

"Yup."

"What you need is a project, an important mission, something to live for."

"Yup. I never had any of that."

"Exactly." Suddenly, I stopped pacing and whirled around to face him. "Ralph, I've never made a habit of giving away free advice or butting into the lives of other dogs."

"That's good."

"But in your case, I'm going to make an exception."

"Uh oh."

"You've made such a mess of your life, you've become such a lout and a slug that I'm going take time out of my busy schedule and help you make something of yourself."

"Now hold on just a minute . . . "

"It won't be easy, Ralph, I'll tell you that up front. But the hardest part was deciding that you wanted to change and do something different with your life."

"Uh huh, but . . . "

"And with that behind us . . . " I walked over and laid a paw on his shoulder. "I just happen to have the perfect deal for you, Ralph, a top-secret mission to save a lady in distress."

"I'm kind of busy."

"And her four lovely children . . . "

"Need to catch up on my sleep."

" . . . from a gangster-dog named Rambo. Congratulations, Ralph. You've been chosen, out of all the dogs in Twitchell, to take part in this mission."

He rolled his sad eyes around on me. "You're awful pushy."

"She's my sister, Ralph."

"That's my name too."

"No, her name is Maggie. Your name is Ralph."

"That sounds better."

"What time does the dogcatcher come to work?"

He yawned. "Oh, first light. Any time now."

"Good, great, excellent. Here's what we're going to do."

I revealed my plan to him. He stayed awake through the whole thing, which was pretty good for Ralph. "He's a Car-Barkaholic, huh? We get a lot of those guys out here. Jimmy Joe can't stand a car-barking dog."

"That's perfect, couldn't be better. As soon as we hear Jimmy Joe coming down the road, we'll take off."

"Sure sounds like a lot of trouble."

"Yes, Ralph, but there's a reward in it for you."

His ears jumped up. "Oh yeah? Well, that's a different deal. I thought maybe you was just mooching off of a friend."

I chuckled at that. "Not at all, Ralph. This reward will be something special."

I didn't have time to tell him that his reward would be waiting for him in heaven, because at that very moment my ears picked up the sound of a vehicle coming down the caliche road.

CHAPTER
11

ATTACKED ON THE STREET BY RAMBO

Sure enough, it was Jimmy Joe Dogcatcher, coming to work, and the moment had arrived to put our plan into action. I nosed open the cell door and went zooming away from Death Row.

Ralph followed — slowly. "Ralph, you're going to have to pick up the pace."

"I'm a-tryin'."

"After all, this is a paying job. We expect you to perform as a professional."

"My legs are awful short, and I might be a smidgeon overweight."

"We're not interested in excuses, Ralph, just an honest day's work for an honest day's pay."

"Could we talk some more about the pay?"

"We're out of time for questions, Ralph, sorry."

"Oh shucks."

We loped away from the dog pound, heading west and north towards town. When we passed Jimmy Joe Dogcatcher's pickup, he slammed on his brakes, jumped out, and started yelling.

"Ralph, come here, boy! Ralph! Why you flop-eared idiot, come here!"

That was our cue to pick up the pace. We moved from a lope to a gallop. That made Jimmy Joe mad, as I knew it would, and he started yelling and fuming and jumping up and down. We kept running. Jimmy Joe jumped back into his pickup,

G.L. Holmes

spun around in a half-circle, and came roaring down the road after us.

I must admit — this might come as a shock, so prepare yourself — I must admit that I experience a certain wicked pleasure in running away from someone who's calling me. I know that sounds awful, but it's true, and the madder and louder the caller gets, the more I feel that exhilarating rush of . . . something.

Power. Glory. Freedom. Independence.

Maybe you have to be a dog to understand how much fun it is to be a naughty dog, but take my word for it: it's one of the greatest thrills this old life has to offer.

I felt it, and so did Ralph. Out of the corner of my eye, I could see him grinning — and you don't see basset hounds doing that very often.

"Hey Ralph, you're grinning. What's the deal?"

"Oh, it's kind of fun to get chased by the dog-catcher again. It's been a long time."

"See, what did I tell you? You've been missing out on the best of Life's experiences."

"I reckon so, if Jimmy Joe don't wring my neck for running off."

"Don't dwell on the little things, Ralph. It's your neck and you have a right to do with it what you wish."

"Yeah, but I don't need to get it wrung."

By that time we had come to Main Street. Crossing a busy street was no big deal for me. I just waited for a break in the traffic and darted across to the other side.

But it wasn't so easy for Ralph. If you recall, he had mentioned something about his short legs. That had been no exaggeration. He did in fact have short legs, and "darting" across streets wasn't something he did particularly well.

With his short basset legs and compact body, and with his complete lack of ambition, Ralph never darted anywhere. He *walked* out into the middle of the street and stood there while cars went whizzing past. Several of them had to swerve to miss him, and they honked their horns.

And Jimmy Joe Dogcatcher was closing in on us. I yelled, "Ralph, get out of the dadgum street and come on! We've got things to do and places to go."

He came clicking across to the other side, and that grin I had noticed before had gotten bigger. "Boy, I'd almost forgot how much fun it was to stop traffic. I may never sleep again."

"Have fun on your own time, Ralph. We've got a job to do."

We left Main Street and headed west. When we came to the first alley, we made a right turn. Jimmy Joe Dogcatcher did the same. He was getting closer. We sprinted several blocks down the alley. I could hear him yelling at Ralph over the roar of the pickup motor.

When we came to the end of the second or third block, I don't remember which, we left the alley, cut across an unfenced yard, and made our way to the street that ran between and in front of two rows of houses.

We gained a little ground on Jimmy Joe by cutting across the yard, but he was still behind us. And still mad. In other words, my plan was working to perfection. Now, all I had to do was lead him past the house where Rambo stayed.

Oops, I sort of revealed my plan there, but I guess it would be all right to declassify some of the details at this point. I couldn't reveal it sooner because I couldn't risk blowing the mission, don't you see.

Okay, here's the plan, but you have to promise not to tell anyone. Promise? Here goes.

Phase One required that I recruit Dog-Pound Ralph for the assignment, because without success on Phase One, there would have been no Phase Two.

Phase Two called for Ralph and me to run away from the dog pound, timing our departure so that we would pass Jimmy Joe Dogcatcher just as he came to work.

Phase Three was a little riskier than the others because control of this phase passed out of my control, so to speak. The Master Plan called for Jimmy Joe Dogcatcher to chase Ralph into town.

Let me pause here. If you're keeping score on this mission, you should have made checkmarks beside Phases One, Two, and Three, unless your book belongs to the library and then you'd better keep your checkmarks to yourself, lest the librarian catch you and put checkmarks on your fanny.

Beware of angry librarians.

Anyways, we had passed through Phases One, Two, and Three and had cleared them all. All that remained was Phase Four, the most important of all. Our primary objective in Phase Four was to . . . well, you're fixing to find out.

We were running down the street, see, with the dogcatcher right behind us. This was new territory for me — the street-side of the neighborhood. I knew the alley-side fairly well because I had always been an alley-and-backyard kind of dog myself, never had spent much time fooling around in front yards and front porches.

And let me tell you something. The world changes when you go from the back alley to the front street. I mean, you go from trash cans and weeds and unpainted fences, to neat yards and clean porches and house fronts that have been painted and kept up.

It's the same world but it sure doesn't look the same.

Well, we sprinted down the street until we came to a small, junky-looking house in the middle of the block. I had a feeling that this might be the place.

And when I heard a double-clutching diesel truck come roaring out of the backyard, I KNEW it was the right place. It wasn't actually a diesel truck, see, just looked like one and sounded like one.

It was Rambo. He came loping out of Maggie's backyard like a big racehorse, and his bark rattled windows all over the neighborhood.

"A-ROOF, A-ROOF, A-ROOF-A!!"

That bark not only rattled windows, it rattled me, especially when I noticed that Rambo's ears were up and his eyes were aimed in my direction.

Ralph was a few steps behind me, and he too saw what was coming our way. "Holy cow, is that a big dog or a little horse?"

"That's the guy we're going to take out, Ralph."

"Not if I have a heart attack, we won't."

"Don't have a heart attack, Ralph. We've reached the most critical phase of the entire mission."

"If that dog catches up with us, we'll both be critical."

"Just keep running, Ralph, we've almost ... "

WHOMP!

Rambo was faster than I had supposed. I mean, you watch a Great Dane loping along and he doesn't appear to be covering much ground. What you tend to forget is that each one of those loping strides is about ten feet long.

And all at once he plowed into me and I was rolling down the pavement. "Keep running, Ralph, keep running!"

"Don't you worry about that!" he yelled over his shoulder as he sprinted past.

Rambo started tearing at me before I even stopped rolling. "Say, cowdog, you made a big mistake, coming back on my block, and now I'm fixing to . . . " The dogcatcher's pickup drove past. Rambo's head shot up and his eyes went blank. "A pickup. I've got to have it! I can't stand to see a pickup driving down my street! Let me at 'im!"

I dropped from the deadly grip of his jaws. He lunged out into the street and started chasing the pickup. Dog-Pound Ralph was ahead of him, pumping on those short legs as hard as he could. Rambo didn't even see him, ran right over the top of him, and kept on trucking.

When he caught up with the pickup, he snapped at the back right tire and cut loose with that bark of his: "A-ROOF, A-ROOF, A-ROOF-A!!" The pickup screeched to a halt. The dogcatcher jumped out.

You know, one part of my plan that I hadn't thought out very well was this: Once I had brought Rambo and the dogcatcher together, how was the dogcatcher going to catch him and load him into the cage in the back?

See, if Jimmy Joe wasn't able to catch that huge, ferocious monster of a dog, it would ruin my whole plan. And what if he saw Rambo's size and decided that he had better things to do than tangle with a Great Dane?

I hadn't given that part much thought, and even if I had, it wouldn't have done any good. I had done my part, and the rest was up to Jimmy Joe Dogcatcher.

CHAPTER
12

THE PLAN BACKFIRES
— ALMOST

Jimmy Joe got out and started walking towards Rambo. "Come here, pooch. Let me show you what happens to mutts that bark at my pickup."

Rambo had been trying to bite the tread off the rear tire, but when he saw the dogcatcher come around the back of the pickup, he raised his head and started to growl. Their eyes met and for several seconds they stared at each other. If you recall, Rambo had a pair of smokey eyes that would stop a train.

Jimmy Joe turned and walked back to his pickup, opened the door, and . . . I thought he would jump in and drive away, but he didn't. He reached in and came out with a lariat rope. As quick as a flash, he built a dog-sized loop and went around to the other side of the pickup again.

By the time Rambo saw the rope, it was already too late. Jimmy Joe didn't need but one throw. His hoolihan loop struck like a rattlesnake — whish, snap! And Rambo was a caught dog.

When the loop pulled tight around his neck, his attitude changed 100%. He went from being the neighborhood thug who couldn't be whipped, to just another dumb mutt who had misjudged what a former cowboy could do with a piece of twine.

Jimmy Joe ran the home-end of his rope through the wire at the front of the cage and loaded Rambo just the way you'd load a bawky colt — pulled on the rope and spanked his behind with an elm switch. And fellers, that Great Dane loaded up!

That was a pretty slick piece of cowboy work Jimmy Joe had just pulled off. Even though he and I were on opposite sides of the law, so to speak, I couldn't help but admire the way he handled himself.

But I didn't have much time to think about it, because by that time my neices and nephews arrived on the scene and began smothering me with love, affection, gratitude, congratulations, and so forth. Yes sir, their Uncle Hank had rid the neighborhood of a terrible monster-dog, and by George, they just couldn't say enough good . . . gulk!

HUH?

The, uh, same noose that had snared Rambo seemed to have been tossed in my direction, it appeared, and instead of staying around to celebrate with the kinfolks, I, uh, was more or less dragged — forcibly, bodily, against my will — dragged to the dogcatcher's cage. The cage door flew open, so to speak, and I was pitched inside.

No reading of my rights, no explanation, no ceremony, just pitched inside like an ordinary stray dog.

Well, yikes, the very thought of being pitched into the cage with an angry dog-eating dog who had a grudge to grind was enough to scare the liver right out of me. Fellers, I knew one thing for certain: I didn't need to worry about spending the rest of my life in the Twitchell Dog Pound, because I wouldn't live long enough to get there.

But just before I was mauled and torn to shreds by the awful beast, I made an interesting discovery. The cage was divided in half. I was on one side and Rambo was on the other, with a stout partition between us.

That was real good news.

The dogcatcher pointed a boney finger at me.

"That's for leading Ralph astray, and when we get to the pound, I just might feed you to that pony there." He jerked his head towards Rambo. "It'll cut down my overhead two ways, pooch, and also make the world a better place. Come here, Ralph, you dummy! For running off, you get to ride in the back with the convicts."

And Ralph came flying into the cage with me.

He looked up at me with his big, wet, sad basset-hound eyes. "Well, your plan worked a little too well, I reckon."

"So it appears, Ralph."

"What you going to do now?"

"Well, I'll probably . . . " I turned and cast a glance over to the next cage.

Rambo was staring back at me. "Hi there, cow-dog. Paybacks are a terrible thing."

"I, uh, don't know what you're talking about, and Ralph, I don't suppose there's a secret passageway out of this cage, is there?"

"Well, let me think on that." By this time we were moving down the street. I waited for his answer, and then waited some more. At last it dawned on me that he'd gone to sleep.

"Ralph, we've just turned off of Main Street. We're heading for the dog pound. I don't want to rush you, but my life is hanging in the balance."

His eyes fell open. "Huh? Who am I and where are you? No, I got it backwards. Where am I and who are you?"

"Never mind all of that, Ralph. You were about to tell me about a secret passageway out of this dogcatcher's truck."

"I was, huh? Dogcatcher's truck?"

"That's correct, because if you don't help me escape, I'll be torn to shreds by that Great Dane over in the next pen, and my tragic end will be on your conscience forever and ever. And boy, will you be sorry!"

He shook his head. "You're puttin' too much pressure on me."

We were only about a hundred yards away from the pound. "Yes, I suppose there's an element of truth to that, but I'm feeling a little pressure myself."

"My mind goes blank under pressure. How 'bout yours?"

"No, Ralph, my mind isn't going blank. It's thinking really bad thoughts right now."

We pulled up in front of the pound and stopped. "Ralph, I hate to put it this way, but our friendship is on the line. If you don't tell me about that secret passageway — and do it very soon — you're going to lose a valuable friend."

"Boy, I'd hate that."

"Now, quickly, tell me about the secret passageway out of here."

"Okay." He yawned. "Far as I know, there ain't one."

Our eyes met. "What do you mean, there ain't one?"

"I mean there ain't a secret passage, is what I mean. What kind of dogcatcher would build a secret passage into his truck?"

"I can't answer that question, Ralph. My mind goes blank under pressure."

"Yeah, mine too. I just hate it when that happens."

Jimmy Joe had walked around to the cage door and was fumbling with his keys. Rambo was grinning at me and licking his chops. Jimmy Joe opened the door and snapped his fingers at me.

"Come on, pooch, this is the end of the road for you."

Suddenly it occurred to me that a program of non-violent non-cooperation might work here. If I laid down at the back of the cage and refused . . . but on the other hand, I hadn't known about his stick with the hook on the end, or that he could slip that hook around my neck and drag me . . .

I was caught. There would be no secret pass-age, no way out, no happy ending. I would be torn to shreds in the line of duty. Never again would I roll in the sewer or bark at the mailman or wake up to the fresh sage-scented air on my beloved ranch. Never again . . .

Another pickup drove in and stopped. A tall, skinny, cowboy-looking fellow stepped out, stuffed his hands into his pockets, and ambled over. There was something familiar about the way he . . .

Holy smokes, IT WAS SLIM!

"Morning," he said to Jimmy Joe. "Looks like you found my dog. I didn't know he'd come to town with me, but I'm thinkin' maybe he did."

"Yeah? Well, you can sure have him back."

"I'd appreciate it."

Slim reached for me but the dogcatcher pulled away. "Not so fast, pardner. No tags, no collar, no shots, no leash, barking at cars, and making a public nuissance. This dog's worth about $145, the way I figger it."

Slim swallowed. "You take checks?"

"Not from cowboys."

"That makes sense." Slim lifted his hat and scratched his head. "You caught any good fish lately?"

G. L. Holmes

"Nah. That old lake's fished out and . . . how'd you know I fish?"

"Oh, just a shot in the dark. You look like the kind of feller who might wet a hook now and then."

"Every weekend, and I haven't caught a decent fish in three months. You know any good places?"

Slim arched his brows and . . . did I see him wink at me? Yes, I was almost sure he did. "Well, yes, now that you mention it, I know several good holes."

Jimmy Joe moved closer. There was a new light in his eyes. "Around here?"

"Uh huh."

"Private land?"

"Yup."

"Catfish or bass?"

"Both."

By this time Jimmy Joe was chewing on his lip and studying old Slim pretty hard. "Where?"

"Heh heh."

"I don't suppose you know the owners, do you?"

"Uh huh, real well."

"Could a guy get written permission to fish?"

"He might, he sure might."

All at once Jimmy Joe set me on the ground and patted my head and gave me a big smile. "Fine dog you've got here, but be more careful the next time you bring him into town, hear? And if you'll just write down the directions to that pond, and sign it, we can all get on about our business."

Slim did the deal and minutes later we were on our way back to the ranch.

Well, what more can I say? I had saved my widowed sister and her kids from a terrible bully, had introduced Dog-Pound Ralph to some of Life's more exciting moments, and had even managed to save my own life at the very last second . . . okay, with a little help from outside sources, but you don't need to spread that around.

Yes, Slim did have a few harsh words for me on the way home, but shucks, that was a small price to pay for another happy ending.

Case closed.